# CROUCHING TIGER

Ying Chang Compestine

*illustrated by* Yan Nascimbene

CANDLEWICK PRESS

MY GRANDPA was coming to visit,
all the way from China. When he arrived,
I rushed out to greet him.

"Hello, Grandpa." I bowed, as Mom had
told me to.

"*Ni hao*—hello, Ming Da." Grandpa
mussed my hair.

The next morning, Grandpa was dancing slowly in the garden with his eyes closed. His hands moved like gliding birds. He crouched like a tiger; he drew an invisible bow; he lifted a foot like a rooster and stood still.

Parting the Wild Horse's Mane

I ran outside. "What are you doing, Grandpa?"

He continued his slow dance. I waited until he opened his eyes.

"Good morning, Ming Da. I am practicing tai chi."

"Tai chi?"

"Yes. It is an ancient martial art."

"Oh!" I said. "Like kung fu?"

I showed off my fastest kicks and punches.

Grandpa watched quietly. Feeling my face burn, I stopped.

"Could you teach me, please?" I asked in a low voice.

Grandpa looked straight into my eyes, then nodded slowly.

Grasp Sparrow's Tail

As soon as I got home from school, I ran out to find Grandpa.

"Let's start with the standing meditation," he said. Bending his knees slightly, Grandpa held out his hands as if holding an invisible balloon.

"That's easy!" I copied his position.

Grandpa adjusted my legs. "Focus on your breathing, and clear your mind," he instructed.

Soon my knees grew tired. I started to wobble.

Grandpa put his hands on my shoulders. "Stand steady. Breathe!"

How long did he expect me to do this? My arms felt as heavy as bricks. I dropped my hands.

"Take a short break and then try again," said Grandpa.

Withdraw and Push

As the week passed, I felt cheated. Maybe Grandpa didn't know real kung fu.

"Grandpa, my arms are worn out!" I complained.

"If your arms feel heavy, that shows you need more practice, Ming Da."

Although he spoke English perfectly well with Dad, Grandpa always talked to me in Chinese.

"My name is Vinson, Grandpa."

"Your Chinese name is Ming Da. You are Chinese as well as American," he said firmly.

Draw Bow to Shoot Tiger

On Monday morning, Mom announced that Grandpa would take the bus with me to school.

"But Mom . . ."

"No 'buts,' Ming Da. It will give you a chance to spend more time with Grandpa—and it's on his way to Chinatown."

To avoid talking to him, I read on the bus.

Rollback

Mom picked me up that afternoon. When we got home, Grandpa was still out.

"What's Grandpa doing in Chinatown, Mom?"

"He's training the lion dancers for the New Year parade."

"Is he teaching them how to stand still, too?"

Mom frowned. "No, Vinson. The lion dancers are serious martial arts students. They have been practicing for years."

When Grandpa got home, I hid in my room.

Turn Around and Sweep Lotus with One Leg

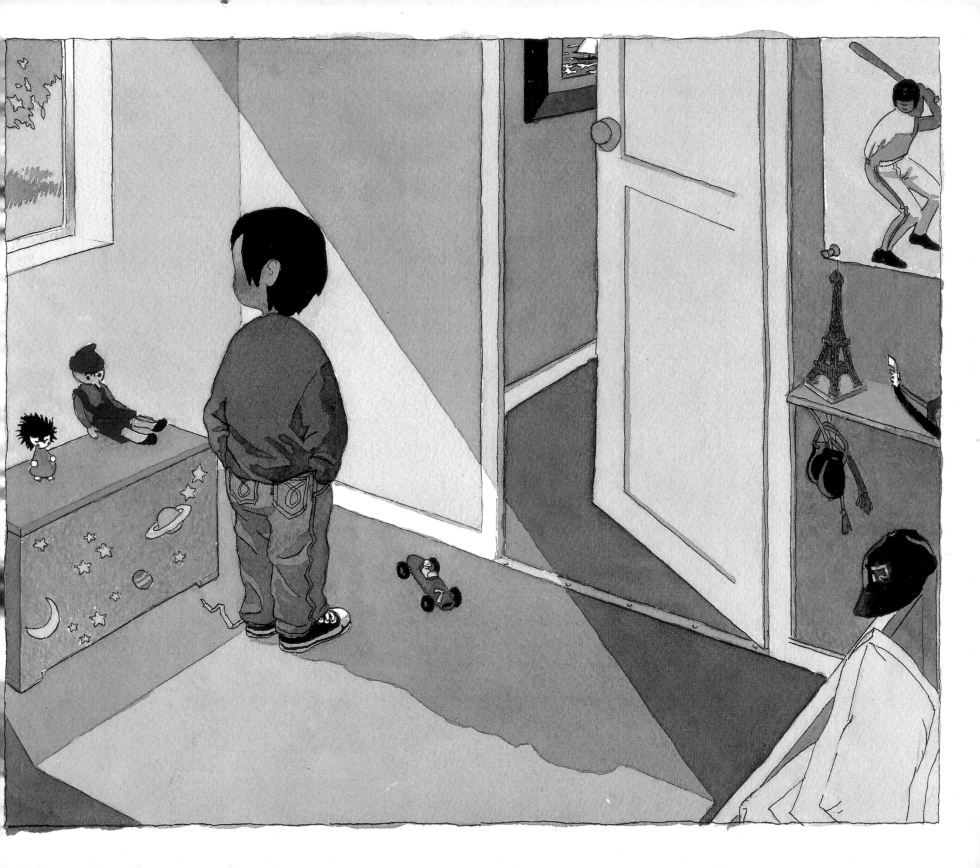

The next morning, on the way to school, I jammed my headphones into my ears to avoid talking to Grandpa. It didn't seem to bother him. He greeted people warmly on the street.

A worker was hauling boards from a truck. A woman rushed past us, talking loudly on her cell phone. Unaware of her, the worker turned, the end of his board speeding toward her head.

In a smooth motion, Grandpa crouched like a tiger, swept up a leg, and kicked the board, breaking it neatly in half.

Play the Pipa

"Wow, Grandpa, how did you do that?" I asked.

He smiled. "Lots of practice—I started at your age."

That night when Grandpa practiced his standing meditation, I joined him.

Single Whip

Over time, I could focus more on my breathing. My legs and arms didn't tire as quickly.

One afternoon, Grandpa put a long bamboo pole into my hands. He taught me the cat walk, keeping my body low and walking slowly, shifting my weight from side to side.

I meditated every day and practiced the cat walk while holding the pole up high. I kept hoping Grandpa would teach me to whack things with the pole. But by the time New Year's came, I still hadn't gotten to hit anything.

Waving Hands in Clouds

On New Year's Eve, we cleaned the whole house. Dad cut my hair, and Mom cooked a big traditional meal. Grandpa handed me a red silk jacket embroidered with dragons. "Ming Da, wear this for the parade tomorrow."

My heart sank. All my friends would be there and see me in this silly jacket. I excused myself and left the table.

Right Heel Kick

When we got to Chinatown, Grandpa took my hand.
"Stay close to me. It will be crowded." I couldn't pull
away from his strong grip. I hoped I wouldn't meet anyone
from school. Shouts and cheers mixed with the crackle of
thousands of firecrackers.

Snake Creeps Through the Grass

Grandpa led me to a pastry stand. *"Ni hao!"* The vendor spoke Chinese with Grandpa so fast I couldn't keep up.

"Such a handsome boy! Here are your favorite pastries," the vendor said. He gave me a bag with meat buns, sesame balls, and coconut cookies inside.

"Thank you! How did you know?"

He smiled and pointed at Grandpa. "He has told me many good things about you. You even study on the bus."

Embarrassed, I avoided Grandpa's eyes.

"Let me pay for these," said Grandpa.

"No, this is my New Year's gift to your grandson." They pushed the money back and forth as if it were on fire.

Finally, the vendor stuffed the money into Grandpa's pocket. "Go, go! The parade starts soon."

Grandpa bowed. I copied him.

Single Pushing Hands

Pushing through the crowd, we met a large group of eager spectators.

"*Ni hao!*" Grandpa greeted them. "This is Ming Da, my grandson."

"*Ni hao!*" they said with big smiles.

I jumped when one of Grandpa's friends thrust a *hóng bāo,* a red envelope that contains money, into my hand. "*Xiè-xiè*—thank you!" I bowed. They chuckled and stuffed more envelopes into my arms.

Grandpa led me through the crowd to the beginning of the parade route.

Needles at Sea Bottom

A group of men wearing jackets just like mine and carrying lion costumes greeted Grandpa warmly.

"Meet my grandson, Ming Da!" Grandpa called out.

"*Ni hao,* Ming Da!" Lion dancers gathered around us. I had never been so close to the lions. I stroked their glistening scales.

"Let's get ready," Grandpa commanded. The lion dancers ducked under their costumes and got into position. Grandpa handed me a long bamboo pole with a cabbage dangling from the top.

"Ming Da, you will be the cabbage boy." He leaned down close to me. "I think you are ready for this role."

My heart jumped with joy.

"Don't let the lions get your cabbage," Grandpa instructed.

I nodded obediently and gripped the pole. Grandpa lit the firecrackers signaling the start of the parade.

Golden Rooster Stands on One Leg

The martial artists led the way. They leaped and whirled about with spears, swords, and other weapons. Grandpa signaled, and I marched off, focusing on keeping the cabbage just out of the lions' reach. People clapped and cheered at the top of their lungs. Many fed the lions *hóng bāo*.

Punch Under Elbow

As we approached the end of the parade, Grandpa yelled, "Ming Da, let the lions have the cabbage!" I lowered the pole. The lions bit at the cabbage and tore it apart, spraying the leaves onto the crowd. I was soaked in sweat and my arms were aching, but my heart was filled with pride.

"Good job! Good job!" Grandpa patted my head.

The martial artists and the lion dancers gathered around us and bowed to Grandpa.

"*Xiè-xiè*. Thank you, Master Chang, for a great parade."

White Crane Spreads Its Wings

When Grandpa and I headed home, it was growing dark. I grabbed his arm. "Grandpa," I said, "I promise I will practice harder."

Grandpa took hold of my hand. "Ming Da, remember that a good martial artist must first gain self-discipline. The standing meditation looks simple, but it builds your inner strength and increases your speed and power."

I nodded.

"To study martial arts is a serious commitment. It takes many years of hard work and dedication." He paused.

I held my breath.

"I believe you have potential."

"Thank you, Grandpa. I promise to do my best!"

Grandpa smiled. "And now," he said, "shall we enjoy those pastries?"

Iron Fan

# AUTHOR'S NOTE

In China, there are two major schools of martial arts: Shaolin and Wudang.

Shaolin was created by Buddhist monks as a form of discipline and defense. It requires external strength and encourages agility and reflexes.

Wudang sprang from the ancient Chinese religion of Taoism. It is a gentle, slow art of movement and breathing, also called tai chi. It stresses the internal skills of stillness. Wudang encourages inner-body strength.

Many Chinese believe that in order to achieve outer strength, one must first gain inner stillness. Tai chi is the foundation of martial arts. Today, tai chi has spread all over the world as a form of exercise rather than for fighting and defense.

Chinese New Year is one of the most important and exciting Chinese holidays. It is a celebration of spring as well as the beginning of a new year. The Chinese lunar calendar determines when it occurs, usually between mid-January and early February. The celebration lasts for fifteen days, with feasts, parades, and fireworks. During this time, children bow to their elders to show their respect. In return, they receive *hóng bāo,* red envelopes containing money.

To ensure a happy and lucky new year, families prepare in many ways. They clean the house to sweep out the old and welcome the new. Children get their hair cut to leave bad luck behind, and they wear new clothes to confuse evil spirits.

GLOSSARY: *hóng bāo* (hong bah-oh): red envelope  *ni hao* (nee how): hello  *xiè-xiè* (shee-eh shee-eh): thank you

In memory of Vinson Ming Da's grandfather Dr. Chang Sin-Liu
Y. C. C.

To Chloé and Julien
Y. N.

Text copyright © 2011 by Ying Chang Compestine
Illustrations copyright © 2011 by Yan Nascimbene

First edition 2011

Library of Congress Cataloging-in-Publication Data is available.

Library of Congress Catalog Card Number 2010048133

ISBN 978-0-7636-4642-4

11 12 13 14 15 16 SCP 10 9 8 7 6 5 4 3 2 1

Printed in Humen, Dongguan, China

This book was typeset in Dante.
The illustrations were done in ink and watercolor.

Candlewick Press
99 Dover Street
Somerville, Massachusetts 02144

visit us at www.candlewick.com